No Mean Street

A hard-hitting play about sex, drugs, and street life

by <u>Paul Boakye</u>

Published by Paul Boakye Associates

Contents

Copyright

PUBLICATION: *No Mean Street* was first published by Alexander Street Press in the United States of America for an academic audience (2003).

ISBN: 978-0-9935389-3-3

The Scenes

The Characters

No Mean Street was first presented by Kuffdem Theatre Company, a Yorkshire based African-Caribbean community theatre group, and Red Ladder; the only Arts Council funded touring theatre company for young people.

ARLINGTON, a man in his late twenties
JEAN, his baby-mother
MARCUS, their eleven-year-old son
DAVID, his friend
STAGGER, a drug-dealer in his late teens
ROSE, a crack addict
A MAN on the Frontline

The Setting

An Inner City

Introduction

When homeboy Arlington is diagnosed as HIV-positive, his reaction is one of disbelief fuelled by fear and prejudice. "That a batty man [gay] disease or you mixed up my blood with a white man's," he says. His words belong to the black community, which denies that Aids is a straight, streetwise man's disease, and the young audience sniggers in recognition.

That acknowledgement is a major breakthrough in Aids education for young black people. Unlike conventional teaching methods, which youth workers feel have made little impact on black teenagers. *No Mean Street* is a powerful, physical drama set in the heart of black street culture speaks their language. "See those leaflets and booklets," said Gillian Gottshalk, a 22-year-old youth worker at The Mill in Bristol, pointing to an information rack after the performance. "This play has made more of an impact than hundreds of those. They don`t mean anything to black teenagers."

Using explicit language, rap music and dance, and populated with the familiar faces of raggas, drug dealers, junkies, homeboys and single parents. *No Mean Street* explodes in enough violence and sexuality to grip the attention of any teenager. Staged close to the audience with Topher Campbell's graphic fast-paced direction, the four black actors hook the audience early using writer Paul Boakye's characters to cleverly explore and destroy the popular prejudices and stereotypes which prevent black teenagers taking the dangers of HIV and Aids seriously.

By following Arlington's fall from arrogant homeboy to abandoned outcast with HIV, the audience is made to question their own preconceptions. Was Arlington so cool? Is safe sex such a bad idea? Wasn't he a better father and boyfriend after he accepted he was HIV? If he can get it, perhaps? These themes form the basis of post-performance workshops where the audience, normally aged between 13 and 25, share their experiences and opinions of the play with the actors.

At the Mill Youth Centre in the "crack city" area of Bristol, a sussed 15-year-old was criticising boys` attitudes to condoms. "There's nothing wrong with girls carrying condoms, but boys call you a slut," she said.

A cheeky teenage boy with a baby on his lap was questioning one of the character's reactions to HIV, "You should stick with your woman or man if they had HIV not tell them to get out," he insisted.

In a separate workshop, youth workers expressed surprise that despite most of the audience having never stepped foot in a theatre, they were gripped. "We need more of this," said Bev McFarque. In the three years, she had been at The Mill it was the only theatre they had been offered.

But then *No Mean Street* is the first nationally targeted Aids project for black youth. Presented by Kuffdem Theatre Company, a Yorkshire based African-Caribbean community theatre group, and Red Ladder, the only Arts Council funded touring theatre company for young people.

The play is part of an HIV/Aids education package for youth centres, Members of Kuffdem and Red Ladder visit centres months before the performance to devise a six-week programme of work involving HIV/Aids workers. Judging by the reaction of the Bristol audience, black youth workers are adamant that theatre is a vital educational tool for black youth and should be adequately funded. "I shouldn't have to wait another three years for something this good," said Bev.

Alison Benjamin
Times Educational Supplement
(London, June 4, 1993)

Scene One
The Blood Test

In a hospital room. The NURSE calls the next patient.

NURSE: Arlington Chase. Arlington Chase.

ARLINGTON: That's me.

NURSE: Right. If you'd like to take a seat.

ARLINGTON: And what's your name?

NURSE: My name's Julie.

ARLINGTON: Julie.

ARLINGTON sits. The NURSE collects her equipment together.

NURSE: Can you roll your sleeves up for me? That's great. Pump your arm.

ARLINGTON does so, and the NURSE ties a Tourniquet tight around

his upper arm.

Oh, you've got small veins, haven't you?

ARLINGTON: Is that good or bad?

NURSE: It's not good. It's not bad. Just makes my job a tad more difficult, that's all. Pump your arm.

The NURSE taps a vein with her finger.

ARLINGTON: Julie, tell me, what time do you get off work?

She pricks him with the needle, and he jumps.

NURSE: Sorry about that. I made you jump, didn't I? Sorry. You can relax your arm now.

The NURSE takes blood samples in two small bottles, removes the needle, and holds cotton wool over the wound.

There you go. All done. Press down on that for me. What's your hospital number?

ARLINGTON: Julie, will you give me your telephone number?

NURSE: You're a bit forward, aren't you?

ARLINGTON: Nothing ventured, nothing gained.

NURSE: Hospital number?

ARLINGTON: M37790

The NURSE writes this on the bottles.

NURSE: Date of birth?

ARLINGTON: 21st August '65.

NURSE: No, press, don't agitate. Would you like a plaster for that?

ARLINGTON: No, too much trouble.

ARLINGTON rolls his sleeve down, and his arm begins to bleed.

NURSE: Look, oh no, you'd better have a plaster, or it won't stop bleeding.

ARLINGTON: Yeah.

NURSE: I know it's a pest when it pulls all the hairs out. But saves your girlfriend the laundry bill.

ARLINGTON: What girlfriend?

NURSE: There you go.

ARLINGTON: How about it, Nurse?

NURSE: What? If I was to go out with every man who walks through this hospital, I'd never get any work done. What makes you think I'm interested in you anyway?

ARLINGTON: You telling me you're not?

NURSE: *(Pause)* Okay. If you'd like, come in for your test results on Saturday, make an appointment at reception.

ARLINGTON: Nurse, Julie, I love you.

NURSE: *(Laughs)* You sweet-talking so and so.

ARLINGTON: Take care, yeah?

NURSE: Don't forget to stop off at reception for Saturday.

ARLINGTON: Saturday then. Look, if anything, call me. I'm on my mobile.

ARLINGTON gives her a business card.

At your service. Day and night.

NURSE: *(Smiling)* Ba-bye.

She shakes her head. ARLINGTON exits. Closing the door behind him, he gives a little victory yelp.

Scene Two

Living on the Frontline

**<u>Night. ARLINGTON
moves down the
Frontline. STAGGER
approaches.</u>**

STAGGER: So wha'appen, Arlington, you walking? Weh you car deh?

ARLINGTON: Car in the garage, man.

STAGGER: So you haffe ketch bus?

ARLINGTON: For now.

STAGGER: *(Laughs)* Serve you right, Don. A weh you a do wid dat ole car deh, playing de white man?

ARLINGTON: You know, 'bout car?

STAGGER: What you want, man, is a B.M. Black Man Wagon dat, y'nuh? Good German make car dat. Never give a man a trouble.

ARLINGTON: *(Sucks his teeth)* How much

car me see you have?

STAGGER: Time, man. Time will tell.

ARLINGTON: And pigs will fly. Well, me like my MG Midget, so hush. You know how much money pay for that car? Only twenty-five man in the world have that car, you know. And me have the best one. You see my car, is a investment that. You nuh learn yet all that glitters is not gold.

STAGGER: Only time will tell, Don.

ARLINGTON: Nuh true.

STAGGER: *(Pause)* Bwoy, chuh, nuh money deh 'bout, y'nuh.

ARLINGTON: Recession everywhere, man.

STAGGER: Kyaan mek no money to bloodseed. Fe the whole week is twenty pounds me sell. All week. Chuh! Jah know. Just lick a rock, y'nuh, as well. I wah lick another one, y'see. *(Sucks his teeth)* Lend me some dollars nuh, Arlington, man? Nutten a go down, y'nuh. Trying a runnings an' t'ing but nutten a go down. And like how it hot out here, police deh 'bout, haffe keep moving. An' like how winter come an' it cole. I man hate de cole, y'nuh. Yesterday, hailstone, y'nuh, boss! One lick me pan me ear, y'see. Me seh raatid, a suh Inglan' cole?

ARLINGTON: How much money you want?

STAGGER: Lend me 'bout twenty, t'irty dollars.

ARLINGTON: Me nuh deal in dollars. Thirty pounds you want?

STAGGER: Yeah, man, yeah, man. Dat'll do.

ARLINGTON: I want it back.

STAGGER: Tomorrow, star. *(Pockets the money. Looks around)* See some man inna one gambling house down the Frontline there. Man set up him own little stall fe him crack. Man have him crack pan tray. Another man have him crack pan de gambling table. Fifty man in deh an' all fifty a dem crackman selling crack. They must have people coming direct to dem!

ARLINGTON: You know that.

STAGGER: Must do. One man come in there now to you, the next forty-nine rush him. Me kyaan deal with that, star. So how any dem mek money?

ARLINGTON: Me nuh know!

STAGGER: *(Sucks his teeth)* An' all a dem smoking crack wid Bunsen Burner going twenty-four seven. Bunsen Burner, y'nuh.

ARLINGTON: Me? No, my yout'! Me smoke my weed. Me have my little stash a weed, but me keep clear a de merchandise, man. Never touch the merchandise. You can't eat inna the profits. Business is business. Even them man like Barry, Pressurefoot and them others you see here selling ... is only death will take them off this Line. Few a them man make good outta the good days on the Line.

Buy them house and settle down an' that. But from day one you see the same faces, and if you don't see them pretty-up, so that you can see ... Just having money counting, counting suh. Money like they never seen in the Bank of England.

STAGGER: Frontline mash-up, man.

ARLINGTON: All the gold rings and ... shit, man! one was there one day, even his dog have a gold teeth in.

STAGGER: Wah dat?

ARLINGTON: He was mad he was. Cokehead. Even his dog have a gold teeth.

STAGGER: Showing off.

ARLINGTON: If he come out the road three times for the day is three suit he's wearing. Three different suit. And he don't walk nowhere. Don't own a car. Chaffer driven everywhere - by minicab.

STAGGER: A joke dat.

ARLINGTON: You know what I'm saying? They call him Gary ... Gary Glitter. The dad was a big vendor. I was there one day when he's putting up rules and leading him customers, telling them "This is my son, Gary! Check my son, Gary!" As though it's a big thing. The boy mad! Was in a mental institution. Dirty now, too, I hear. All them lifestyles, man, and for what?

STAGGER: You see me, Don, from me born inna Jamaica, me's a yout' wid ambition. Me nuh like go a people yard turn Vampire Bat. One day me will have to be a millionaire. Dollars, man. Dollars a run t'ings now.

ARLINGTON: How you gonna make your millions?

STAGGER: Me a go pull off one skank. Gamble. Me nuh know yet. Every week me go a betting shop. Every week me win somet'ing. One day me nuh mus' get the million. A mus' dat. There's money to be

made, man. Man mek
money.

ARLINGTON: Money make man mad.

STAGGER: Either dat or de pools.

ARLINGTON: You marking the pools?

STAGGER: No.

ARLINGTON: *(Laughs)* Yeah, Stagger.
Right. I see you later, man.

STAGGER: Weh you gone? Stop an' chat
nuh, man.

ARLINGTON: Got to run, Stagger, man.
Got business to do. I catch
you later.

**STAGGER offers a fist
salute. ARLINGTON
offers his outstretched
palm. STAGGER looks
bemused. Just then, a
MAN walks past with a
bicycle.**

STAGGER: You know how much time
dis likkle renk battybwoy a
circle de compound?

ARLINGTON: Him feisty, you see.

STAGGER: Must be looking man dick. Let him come. Me have one big piece a hood fe him.

ARLINGTON: Hold up. Hold up. Let me go check it. Him deh pan the Crack, you know.

MAN: You have anything?

STAGGER: What you want? Ash, coke weed, or crack?

ARLINGTON: Hold it down, Stagger, man. A my customer this still.

ARLINGTON walks towards the MAN as STAGGER'S mobile phone begins to ring.

STAGGER: *(Into phone)* Wha'appen Celia, baby? Yeah, me soon come. Yeah, man, yeah...

MAN: You have a rock?

ARLINGTON: How much you want?

MAN: Give me half an eighth. But is just fifty pounds I have.

ARLINGTON: See't deh.

MAN: Let me look at it.

ARLINGTON: Weh you wah look at my thing fa?

MAN: I wanna see what I'm getting. Man round here sell you sugar cube if you not careful.

ARLINGTON: What you mean? Is my thing this, man.

MAN: I can't buy it if I can't see it.

ARLINGTON: *(Sucks his teeth)* Walk up. Walk up. Round the corner there. Yeah. Right there.

A police siren whizzes past.

See police! That's what I'm trying to avoid. Come, me nuh like too much light. Too much light round here. Come. Move up.

They stop at a corner. ARLINGTON has difficulty opening the small foil-wrapped pellet, drops it, picks it up, and then opens it to

show the MAN.

See't deh.

MAN: That don't look too good to me, you know. Don't you have a weighed piece?

ARLINGTON: Look, you ain't gonna get nothing weighed round here tonight.

MAN: I'll leave it then.

ARLINGTON: Weh you mean - "leave it then"? Look, man, taste it.

MAN: It's all right.

ARLINGTON: See little piece, pan me finger deh, taste it.

The MAN tastes the crack.

What you saying?

MAN: It's all right.

ARLINGTON: Is good shit this, man, don't disrespect my thing.

MAN: I'll leave it, okay.

ARLINGTON: Weh you mek me open my thing fa?

MAN: What's the problem, man? Look, there's plenty people out here selling. You're a seller. I'm a buyer. I need to see what I'm getting.

ARLINGTON: Move from me you likkle pussyhole bwoy before I bus' you head. Weh you mek me open my thing fa?

The MAN moves off with his bicycle, ARLINGTON quickly pockets the pellet of crack, and then shouts after him.

Yow! Look! Look, you make me drop my thing. Find it!

ARLINGTON pretends to search the sidewalk for the crack he's put in his pocket. The MAN approaches STAGGER.

STAGGER: Wha'appen? Ash, coke, weed or crack?

MAN: You have a rock?

STAGGER: Wah you looking?

MAN: You have half an eighth?

STAGGER: Come nuh, man.

MAN: Is forty pounds I have.

STAGGER: My t'ing dem too big fe sell for forty dollars. You have more money? I can do you a nice piece for fifty.

MAN: That's all I have.

STAGGER: Come, man, come. Me and you can sort something out. Have a look at it. Taste it.

MAN: Nice.

The MAN removes money from his jacket pocket and pays STAGGER. ARLINGTON approaches from behind.

ARLINGTON: Is weh him a do? Get you fe show him you stuff then he don't want it?

STAGGER: Is dat what he did?

STAGGER grabs the MAN and holds him as ARLINGTON approaches.

MAN: Another time, man? I'm always round here. I'll see you another time.

ARLINGTON: What other time to bloodseed? A going kill you!

STAGGER grabs a brick, takes a swing at the MAN; the MAN blocks the brick with one hand, whilst holding his bicycle with the other.

MAN: What's the matter with you? Let go a me, man.

ARLINGTON: You nuh see you mek me drop my stuff. How me going find it fe sell it now?

STAGGER: Tief his bike.

MAN: I'm sorry.

STAGGER: Tief his bike.

ARLINGTON tries to pull the bike from under

MAN, the MAN holds onto the bike, still trying to block STAGGER taking another swing with the brick.

MAN: Let go a me, man. I'll pay you for it.

STAGGER: I goin' bus' you head.

MAN: I'll pay for it.

STAGGER: He's gonna pay for it.

ARLINGTON: I want my money.

MAN: I can't give you the money 'til you let go a me.

STAGGER and ARLINGTON let the MAN go. The MAN pulls out a wallet from his back pocket. STAGGER snatches the wallet and pulls sixty pounds from it:

STAGGER: Look, he t'ink he's smart. He's telling us he's only got forty dollar when he's got sixty dollars in here. Damn retch!

STAGGER strikes the MAN in the face. The MAN falls to the road and STAGGER is kicking him.

You likkle lying likkle blouse-an-skirt bwoy!

MAN: Wait...

STAGGER: You feisty dog ... you shit ... you cocksucker...

MAN: Stop...

STAGGER: You wah beat man hood? You child molester ... AIDS carrier ... You dirty likkle shit. Don't mess wid me.

STAGGER spits on him.

ARLINGTON: You see that? You see that now? Gimme my money.

MAN: He's got your money.

STAGGER gives ARLINGTON thirty pounds, pockets the rest, and flings the wallet at the MAN in the gutter.

ARLINGTON pulls out a gun from his inside packet pocket, holds it to the MAN'S head.

MAN: No. No. Don't kill me. Please. Don't kill me.

ARLINGTON: You lucky, y'know. You lucky. Run!

The MAN struggles to get up, falls, and turns to pick up his bicycle.

Leave the damn bike! Run!

The MAN staggers off covered in blood. STAGGER and ARLINGTON laugh, touch fist. ARLINGTON picks up the bicycle.

STAGGER: Nice bike this, y'nuh. You t'ink he'll go to police?

ARLINGTON: He won't go to no police.

STAGGER: *(Smiling)* So you carry gun now, star bwoy? You turn Don-Dadda to raas. Let me hol' it nuh.

ARLINGTON shows STAGGER the gun, and he's well impressed.

Pow! Pow! Nice, bwoy, nice. Is one like dis me want. Come, let we walk.

They move down the street. STAGGER'S mobile phone rings. He answers it.

(Into phone) Yow! Who? Celia, baby! Yeah, baby, yeah, baby - wha'appen? Huh-uh. Huh-huh! Arright. Me coming. Me coming. Me have a few dollars now. I coming. *(He hangs up)* Me haffe mek a run, y'nuh, boss. My woman ... when she deh pan de crack ... nutten never sweet suh.

ARLINGTON: Watch yourself, you know, Stagger. This Crack business is a greedy t'ing, y'nuh.

STAGGER: Weh you mean, boss? Me's a yout' wid good sense, y'nuh. Me can handle it, man.

ARLINGTON: All right.

STAGGER: Later, yeah. Bogle's tonight?

ARLINGTON: If I see you, I see you.

ARLINGTON and STAGGER go their separate ways. ARLINGTON has the bicycle.

Scene Three

Bogle's Late-Night Blues

Shady people dance in silhouette. As the music changes tempo from Swingbeat to Bluebeat to Skank to Dub, Bogle, Lovers, and so on, JEAN and ARLINGTON edge closer and closer together until they are dancing Rub-a-Dub style. The music stops.

JEAN: Marcus been asking for you.

ARLINGTON and JEAN leave holding hands.

Scene Four

Jean's Bedroom

JEAN yawns and stretches in bed, sits up and looks expectantly around the room. The eagerness leaves her face when she sees that the room is empty. She yawns and stretches again. A toilet flushes nearby, and the smile returns to her face as ARLINGTON enters dressing to go out. He inspects himself in the mirror, patting aftershave onto his face, and oiling his hair. JEAN yawns and stretches:

ARLINGTON: Hi, you're up.

JEAN: Morning.

ARLINGTON: Afternoon!

JEAN: Is it that late?

ARLINGTON: I have business. Didn't wanna wake you.

JEAN:	Would have been nice to wake up together.
ARLINGTON:	*(Kissing her)* Another time.
JEAN:	No, Arlington. Not another time. Tonight here, like you said. You're taking me out. Or was all that sweet talk last night just to get me into bed?
ARLINGTON:	You're wicked, you know that.
JEAN:	That's not what you were saying last night.
ARLINGTON:	What was I saying? Can't remember a thing.
JEAN:	You'd better. 'Cos if you're coming back into my life, it's got to be on terms we can both live with, 'cos I need a life, and you need to be a father to your son.
ARLINGTON:	Where is he? He's not back yet, you know.
JEAN:	What time is it?
ARLINGTON:	Late. Gone three. You

hungry?

JEAN: He's probably on his own way back from David's by now.

ARLINGTON: Tell him I'll see him later.

JEAN: Should I tell him you'll be around more often from now on?

ARLINGTON: You could tell him that.

JEAN: You know I'm going night school now.

ARLINGTON: Oh, yeah. You doing it then?

JEAN: It's Thursdays six 'til nine. You could take some responsibility for Marcus. Look after him every Thursday night or so.

ARLINGTON: Marcus is a big boy. He can look after himself.

JEAN: I know he can look after himself. But if I'm not careful, he'll be all over the streets, at all hours of the night, and God knows what he'll get up to then. I don't want him following in your footsteps.

ARLINGTON: What's wrong with that?

JEAN: I love you, Arlington. I could never deny that. More fool me. But while you might see yourself as a businessman, I don't know how comes you see a job as something other people do.

ARLINGTON: 'Cos I won't work for no white man. I tried that. I ain't slaving for no one but myself. Selling drugs, selling whatever, is the same supply and demand. The same game. Just the rules are different.

JEAN: Marcus doesn't need a drug dealer for a father.

ARLINGTON: So what do you want me to do about it?

JEAN: You could get a job.

ARLINGTON: Get what job?

JEAN: I don't know. A job. Any job.

ARLINGTON: I'm trying, Jean, man. Don't you see I'm trying. What do you want from me?

JEAN: Oh, I don't know. What's the matter with us?

ARLINGTON: I'm twenty-seven years old. Do you think I like seeing you living in some stinking council flat, with a kid I don't even know and ... and, okay, so it was me, I messed up before ... all them women and thing ... but I got some self-respect, you know, Jean. A man's got to have some self-respect. Still, I'm trying, you know. I'm trying the only way I know how. Last night was good. Last night was very good. But if you expecting me to stop doing what I'm doing, I can't promise you that right now. I got plans.

JEAN: What plans?

ARLINGTON: Just things.

JEAN: Like what?

ARLINGTON: Look, you talk about Marcus.

I understand about Marcus. I know I haven't seen him. I know I haven't been good to you. But he's the extension of me. He's me and you. And one day he's gonna look round, and he's gonna see his old man - a big shot record producer - bigger than Virgin Records. You wait.

JEAN: That's a dream, Arlington.

ARLINGTON: A dream? All right. You wait and see. It's only black people know about music. And it's just the money that's holding me back. I've done the research. I've done everything. It's just the money. The drugs is a means to an end.

JEAN: You just mind you don't get lost in this means to an end.

ARLINGTON: Trust me, man. Trust me.

JEAN: I don't want no trouble at my door.

ARLINGTON: Relax. I got my own place. You think I'd do anything to harm you and Marcus?

JEAN: Have you changed that much?

ARLINGTON: Wait and see.

JEAN: What time will I see you tonight?

ARLINGTON: Latish. About ten, eleven, or so. I got some things to finish off.

JEAN: Where're you taking me?

ARLINGTON: Surprise.

JEAN: Don't give me no card now, you know, Arlington.

ARLINGTON: Think of a place you want to go. Some place nice.

JEAN: And when you say eleven o'clock, knowing the blackness of time, I ain't waiting around all night.

ARLINGTON: Trust me.

JEAN: There might just be some other man I want to go out with tonight.

ARLINGTON: I'll kill him.

She laughs. ARLINGTON removes a wad of money from his pocket.

Here. Give this to Marcus. Tell him to buy himself something.

JEAN: If you wanna get him something take him to the shop and buy it yourself. Don't give it to me.

ARLINGTON: What about you? You have a nice dress for tonight?

JEAN: Keep your money.

ARLINGTON: Come on, baby, buy yourself something.

JEAN: I don't want your drug money, Arlington. You got to stop this living.

ARLINGTON: I will. I promise.

JEAN: Can I believe you?

ARLINGTON: Wait and see.

JEAN:	I must be mad.
ARLINGTON:	I got to go. I see you later.
	<u>ARLINGTON blows her a kiss and exits.</u>
JEAN:	He'll be sorry he missed you.

Scene Five

On the Street, Outside Jean's Flat

MARCUS is riding a 'too-small' BMX bike. DAVID approaches.

DAVID:	Hey, Marcus!
MARCUS:	Don't shout out my name, man - what?
DAVID:	You'd never guess what?
MARCUS:	What?
DAVID:	She's taken by a dog.
MARCUS:	What?
DAVID:	Joke! She's taken by a boy called Steve.
MARCUS:	Are they still looking?
DAVID:	I can't see.
MARCUS: looking?	Do you think they're still
DAVID:	I dunno.

MARCUS:	Go and chat to them again.
DAVID:	What for, man? I just told her … *(In a girl's voice)* … my mate fancies you!
MARCUS:	Go and ask her her name.
DAVID:	She says her name is Susan.
MARCUS:	Susan? Susan what? Go and ask her her surname. Ask her what school she goes to.
DAVID:	She goes to Burnt Hole.
MARCUS:	Burnt Ash, you fool! Tell her, I want her.
DAVID:	What for?
MARCUS:	Tell her to come chat to me.
DAVID:	Girls don't chat-up boys. You go and tell her. You should see her as well. She's so ugly and white.
MARCUS:	Don't you like her?
DAVID:	She's a dog, man. She looks like AIDS.

MARCUS:	You going?
DAVID:	I'm gone. See you later. Woof! Woof!
MARCUS:	You wait.
	MARCUS jumps off his bike and pretends to shoot DAVID. DAVID fires back and exits. MARCUS gets back on the bicycle and rides in circles. ROSE approaches.
	Are you looking for my dad?
ROSE:	I'm looking for Arlington. Do you know where he is?
MARCUS:	He's my dad.
ROSE:	Is he really? Is he in?
MARCUS:	He don't live here no more.
ROSE:	Since when?
MARCUS:	Only I and my mum live here now.
ROSE:	Oh!

MARCUS:	Do you want me to take you to him?
ROSE:	Could you?
MARCUS:	I gotto go in the shop.
ROSE:	Where is he?
MARCUS:	Crawley Estate.
ROSE:	Where's that?
MARCUS:	Do you want me to take you to him?
ROSE:	Yeah, okay.
MARCUS:	This way.

MARCUS removes a packet of crisp from his pocket.

Do you want one?

ROSE:	No. You have them. *(Pause)* You should get your dad to buy you a big bike.
MARCUS:	This isn't mine. I've got a big bike. It's being fixed. This way. Do you know Crawley Estate?

ROSE:	No.
MARCUS:	It's near Myatt's Field.
ROSE:	Okay.
MARCUS:	Cross over at the lights.

<u>They stop then walk off in silence.</u>

Scene Six

*Ghetto Heaven, Outside a
Crack Estate*

**<u>ARLINGTON is sipping a
beer. STAGGER is beside
him. They stand for a
while.</u>**

ARLINGTON: I see Cooper.

STAGGER: Which Cooper?

ARLINGTON: Your friend, the hairdresser.

STAGGER: Weh him seh? Him seh
anyt'ing 'bout de job?

ARLINGTON: What job?

STAGGER: Him did have a job for me,
y'nuh. Weh you see him?

ARLINGTON: Up a Chapel Town.

STAGGER: Where? In de park?

ARLINGTON: How you know?

STAGGER: Must be up there practising
his obsession. Hear seh him
have a nice piece a t'ing up

there, y'nuh.

ARLINGTON: What, a Browning?

STAGGER: Yes, Don. Nice young brown t'ing. Hear seh de t'ing love perform.

ARLINGTON: Bwoy, I hate a performance.

STAGGER: Hear seh de t'ing love exhibition, man.

ARLINGTON: *(Sucks his teeth)*

STAGGER: Hear seh if you blind-fold a man, put him in deh, he'd t'ink seh is de natural t'ing him deh in.

ARLINGTON: What?

ROSE: *(Approaching)* Is this it?

MARCUS: *(Approaching)* Yeah.

STAGGER: People a come.

MARCUS: Look over there if you see him. I'm just checking to see if he's over here.

STAGGER: Weh you a seh, my yout'? Ash, Crack, Weed or Coke?

MARCUS: Stagger, it's me, Marcus. Have you seen my dad?

STAGGER: See him deh.

ARLINGTON: Marcus, what do you want?

MARCUS: Hello, dad.

ROSE: Arlington, darling, is that you? It's me, Rose, how are you?

STAGGER: Hey, gyal, come. Long-time me and you nuh do a t'ing.

ROSE: Get off me!

STAGGER: Since six months come. I want my t'ing now.

ROSE: Get off me, Stagger! Arlington, help! Call off your maaga dog.

ARLINGTON: Hol' it down nuh, Stagger, man.

MARCUS: Arright, dad?

ARLINGTON: Ey? Is you walk her here?

MARCUS: Yeah.

STAGGER:	See you bodyguard deh. You looking after you father?
MARCUS:	Yeah.
STAGGER:	Look after him, cos if he never look after you, you wouldn't reach dat age.
ARLINGTON:	What you doing here? Go home.
ROSE:	Don't be hard on him, darling, he was only helping.
MARCUS:	Dad, can I buy a drink on the way?
ROSE:	Give him something, Arlington. Please, just for me. I would if I had it.
ARLINGTON:	*(To ROSE and STAGGER)* 'Scuse me a minute.

ARLINGTON takes MARCUS aside. Takes out a wad of notes, gives him some.

Here. Go on. Don't spend it all at once. And I don't let me see you round here again.

MARCUS: Thanks, dad. You gonna come by and see us soon?

ARLINGTON: I'll see you tonight.

MARCUS: Is that a promise then, dad?

ARLINGTON: What did I say?

MARCUS: Nice one, dad.

ARLINGTON: Go on. Button up your Anorak.

MARCUS: Okay.

STAGGER: A your pikney dat, Arlington.

ARLINGTON: See't deh.

STAGGER: Nice little bwoy dat. Bwoy favour you, y'nuh.

ARLINGTON: He have a weak chest from birth. Catch cold easy. I keep telling him to mind himself, but he look out for me, y'know.

ROSE: He's a lovely kid. You know, Arlington, I've got no kids. Can't have none now either. But I've had two abortions.

Yes, I have had two
abortions.

ARLINGTON: Rose, where have you been?
I was wondering the other
day where you were.

ROSE: Been in Holloway Prison six
months. Met up with all old
friends. You knew Beverley,
didn't you, Arlington?

ARLINGTON: Beverley?

ROSE: Her name was Hyacinth, but
everybody called her
Beverley, on account of she
didn't smell too sweet.

ARLINGTON: *(Laughing)* That's right.

ROSE: *(Seducing him)* You know,
Arlington, Beverley always
had the hots for you, though,
don't you? Oh yeah, did that
girl have the hots for you,
boy. Couldn't cope with it, of
course. Said you were a no-
good womanizer. Ha, ha, ha,
ha, haaaaa! Mad on you she
was. Mad on you. Couldn't
resist you in fact. Ha, ha, ha!

STAGGER: Gyal, look good, though,

eeeh?

ROSE: *(Showing off her body)* Six months in Holloway, darling, recommend it to anyone. I feel completely alive again.

STAGGER: Weh you want? You wah rock?

ROSE: You have a rock?

STAGGER: See't deh. Gimme the money.

ARLINGTON: Stagger, this is my customer, man.

ROSE: I am his customer, Stagger.

STAGGER sucks his teeth.

ARLINGTON: What you looking?

ROSE: Well, Arlington, darling, I didn't get my giro today, you know. Went down to the DSS they said come back next Wednesday. That's why I came all this way to see old friends.

ARLINGTON: I don't think so, y'know, Rose.

ROSE: Oh no! Why not? Baby, go on. Pleeeeeeeaseeeee!

ARLINGTON: Times are hard.

ROSE: You can do it for me, though?

STAGGER: *(Holding a rock)* Is this you want?

ROSE: Oh, Stagger, go on. How many favours have I done you?

STAGGER taunts her with the foil-wrapped pellet. ROSE grabs at it, misses at first, gets it, opens the packet, finds something, examines it, and bites it.

ROSE: Stagger, you wicked, bastard! It's chalk! It's bleeding chalk. Arlington, Stagger, please. I beg you. You know I'm a good customer when I'm in circulation.

STAGGER: Me want my t'ing now.

ROSE: Arlington, you do it. Go on,

please. Just a few days credit. Please, darling. You know I'd do my thing with you any time.

STAGGER: *(Grabbing her by the throat)* Gyal, you nuh hear weh me seh? Me seh come!

ROSE: No need to be so difficult. He's so rough this one. And I know exactly what he likes as well.

STAGGER: Come!

ROSE: All right!

STAGGER drags her aside and bends her over a wall face down.

STAGGER: Come nuh, Arlington, man - you nuh wah piece?

ROSE: If it's two of you, it's two rocks I want. Okay. No need to push. What's your problem?

STAGGER: Arlington, come.

ARLINGTON: Me's a big man, me nuh like watch dog anyhow.

ARLINGTON exits.

ROSE: Don't suppose you have a condom, do you?

STAGGER: Condom? Condom don't fit me, man. Weh you wah condom fa? You have AIDS?

ROSE: Bleeding check! What do you think I am? I ain't a whore, you know. I'm just doing this 'cos I need a wrap.

STAGGER: Shut up!

STAGGER pushes her face down and unzips his jacket.

Scene Seven

The Diagnosis

<u>ARLINGTON and the COUNSELLOR face one another.</u>

COUNSELLOR: And so, do you normally practice safer-sex?

ARLINGTON: Do I practice what?

COUNSELLOR: Do you normally use a condom?

ARLINGTON: Man, I don't like them things, y'know.

COUNSELLOR: But a condom could stop you picking up sexually transmitted diseases like Gonorrhoea.

ARLINGTON: That's just life, man, ennit. You come here now, you take the Penicillin, it clear it up.

COUNSELLOR: You were diagnosed has having Gonorrhoes. That's why it was suggested you take an HIV test. Don't you worry about AIDS?

ARLINGTON: AIDS? AIDS is a battyman disease.

COUNSELLOR: AIDS is not a gay disease.

ARLINGTON: What is it then?

COUNSELLOR: AIDS is a series of illnesses caused by a virus, which can infect anybody if it enters the bloodstream. AIDS isn't a black disease, it isn't a gay disease.

ARLINGTON: So? So what's that got to do with me?

COUNSELLOR: You took an HIV-test.

ARLINGTON: Yeah.

COUNSELLOR: Your results came back yesterday.

ARLINGTON: And?

COUNSELLOR: Well, I'm afraid you're HIV-positive.

ARLINGTON: What?

COUNSELLOR: You have the virus that can cause AIDS.

ARLINGTON: Uh-uh, man, that ain't right. I don't know which white man's blood you got mixed up there with mine, but that ain't my blood right, 'cos as far as I'm concerned, black people don't get AIDS.

COUNSELLOR: What about Magic Johnson?

ARLINGTON: I don't care about Magic Johnson.

COUNSELLOR: I know this must come as a shock to you, Arlington, but it might be a good idea to take one or two leaflets away with you.

ARLINGTON: Look, I've read the leaflets, man, I know. I've read the papers too, all right. They say people who get HIV get AIDS and they die.

COUNSELLOR: That isn't entirely certain

ARLINGTON: So, what you telling me? You telling me that people who get HIV get AIDS and they don't die? Is that what you're telling me?

COUNSELLOR: I'm saying people with HIV don't necessarily go on to develop AIDS.

ARLINGTON: HIV ... virus ... AIDS ... safer-sex ... if what you're saying is true, how long have I got to live with this shit?

COUNSELLOR: We don't know.

ARLINGTON: So what are you doing here, then?

COUNSELLOR: I'm here to give you help and advice. AIDS is just a disease, and like any other disease, you can fight it.

ARLINGTON: But you ain't giving me no answers, man, you ain't saying nothing to me.

COUNSELLOR: I've been HIV-positive for the past seven and a half years. I don't have the answers. I just eat well, sleep well, avoid stress, and take regular check-ups.

ARLINGTON: You have it too?

COUNSELLOR: Yes.

ARLINGTON: Are you...?

COUNSELLOR: No, I'm straight. Do you have a girlfriend?

ARLINGTON: Yeah.

COUNSELLOR: Children?

ARLINGTON: I got a son.

COUNSELLOR: How old?

ARLINGTON: Eleven.

COUNSELLOR: Difficult at that age, aren't they? Is it just the one girlfriend?

ARLINGTON: What's that supposed to mean?

COUNSELLOR: Are there any others? Do you have names?

ARLINGTON: I don't remember names, okay.

COUNSELLOR: Well, I strongly recommend that your girlfriend comes in for an HIV test.

ARLINGTON: Jean? Jean might have it?

COUNSELLOR:	I stress, it's only a precautionary measure.
ARLINGTON:	Shit! How did I get it, man, that's what I wanna know?
COUNSELLOR:	There are only four ways of passing on the HIV virus: One, through penetrative sex without a condom, two, through infected blood and blood products, three, by re-using needles or syringes, and four, from mother to child at birth.
ARLINGTON:	No, man, what I mean is, who gave it to me?
COUNSELLOR:	If you could pinpoint one person, would that make you feel better?
ARLINGTON:	I'd kill her.
COUNSELLOR:	Isn't it just as important to think how many people you might have given it to?
ARLINGTON:	Am I supposed to feel embarrassed or something? Am I supposed to feel guilty for not wearing a condom? Am I?

COUNSELLOR: I know this must be a very difficult time for you, Arlington. Would you like me to arrange for you to see a counsellor at our specialist HIV-unit?

ARLINGTON: Look, just don't talk to me, all right. You people don't know nothing 'bout nobody's health. So what if I've got this HIV? What can you do about it? You people don't know shit!

ARLINGTON storms out.

Scene Eight
Dream of a Happy Family

<u>JEAN is studying;
MARCUS is seated at the
dining table:</u>

MARCUS: Mum.

JEAN: What, Marcus? I'm busy.

MARCUS: You know David?

JEAN: Yes.

MARCUS: He says if you don't have a dad, you'll turn out a battyman.

JEAN: Marcus, don't use that word. Where did he get that from?

MARCUS: That's what his mum and dad said.

JEAN: Well, it's not true. Lots of people don't have dads. I don't think it makes them homosexual.

MARCUS: What's homosexual?

JEAN:	When a man likes another man.
MARCUS:	Like I like David, do you mean?
JEAN:	Not like that, Marcus.
MARCUS:	How then? Am I homosexual?
JEAN:	No, you're not. Homosexual means the same as battyman, but battyman isn't a nice word. The proper word is gay.
MARCUS:	Gays get AIDS, don't they?
JEAN:	Marcus, will you stop that stupid talk right now. Anyone can get AIDS. Don't they teach you anything at school? I'll soon stop you seeing that David if that's what his parents are telling him. Now be quiet, I'm busy.
MARCUS:	What are we having for dinner?
JEAN:	What do you want?
MARCUS:	Fried eggs and peaches.

JEAN: Marcus, you can have fried eggs, then you can have peaches with your ice cream.

MARCUS: But I want fried eggs and peaches.

JEAN: Marcus, you can't eat fried eggs and peaches.

MARCUS: Why not? I want bacon, fried eggs and peaches.

JEAN: You want bacon, fried eggs and peaches?

MARCUS: Yeah.

JEAN: Okay, then.

MARCUS: And some bread.

JEAN: And you better eat it all.

MARCUS: Brilliant.

JEAN: And don't be sick either.

MARCUS: Mmmmm.

JEAN: So, what else did David say?

MARCUS: I'm not telling you.

JEAN: No, no, go on.

MARCUS: I'm still not telling you.

JEAN: Why not?

MARCUS: He's my good friend.

JEAN: Oh, I see, a man of principles. *(Pause)* Well, your dad came round today.

MARCUS: Uh-huh.

JEAN: He's moving back.

MARCUS: Moving back, where?

JEAN: Here, silly. He's coming back to live with us.

MARCUS: For good?

JEAN: Uh-uh. *(Pause)* Aren't you happy? *(Pause)* It'll be like old times again. Me, you and your dad. Won't it, ey?

MARCUS: Mmmmmmm.

JEAN: *(Pause)* We can go out and do all the things we used to do.

MARCUS: *(Long pause)* Are you happy, mum?

JEAN: Yeah, of course, I am. Why? Are you?

MARCUS: I'm happy.

JEAN: Are you sure?

MARCUS: Yeah.

JEAN: Give me a hug.

MARCUS hugs her, starts to leave.

Where are you going?

MARCUS: I'm going up to tidy my room.

MARCUS exits, JEAN stands thinking.

Scene Nine

The Breakdown

ARLINGTON and MARCUS seated on the settee in Jean's living room. ARLINGTON is rolling a joint and drinking beer. MARCUS secretly copies his dad's every move. ARLINGTON lights the joint. MARCUS pretends to smoke a pencil. He stops when ARLINGTON looks at him and starts again when he turns away. They repeat this cat and mouse game until ARLINGTON catches MARCUS out and slaps the pencil from his mouth. MARCUS smiles naughtily, then, he knocks the joint from ARLINGTON'S hand. ARLINGTON moves to slap him but changes his mind.

ARLINGTON: Go to your room!

MARCUS recoils in terror.

I said, go to your room!

MARCUS picks up the joint and hands it to his father. ARLINGTON looks at the joint, and then at his son, he takes the joint. MARCUS leaves the room. ARLINGTON flops onto the settee, hesitates over the joint in his hand, and then takes another puff. Pause. We hear keys in the door as JEAN enters with shopping bags.

JEANS: What happened to you last night?

ARLINGTON: You all right?

JEAN: Where were you?

ARLINGTON: Hmm?

JEAN: You heard me.

ARLINGTON: I had some things to do. I'm sorry.

JEAN: And you couldn't phone me?

ARLINGTON: I'm sorry.

JEAN: Left me sitting here waiting all night like an idiot. What is it, another woman?

ARLINGTON: It's not another woman, Jean.

JEAN: I ain't going back to that, Arlington.

ARLINGTON: I said I'm sorry, okay. I'm sorry. How many times do I have to say it? It won't happen again.

JEAN: Huh! *(Pause)* I'm cooking soup. Do you want some?

ARLINGTON: No, thanks.

JEAN: Something to drink?

ARLINGTON: No, I'm fine.

JEAN: Are you sure?

ARLINGTON: I'm not hungry.

JEAN: *(Sitting down and touching*

him) You look a bit off colour. What's the matter?

ARLINGTON: You know how it is. Tough but just have to hold it together.

JEAN: So, what happened last night?

ARLINGTON: Hmm?

JEAN: You didn't go and see one of your girlfriends then?

ARLINGTON: Jean, man, it's not like that any more.

JEAN: Is everything okay?

ARLINGTON: Yeah. Fine. Everything's fine. I'm interrupting you, ennit?

JEAN nestles her head on ARLINGTON'S chest, he flinches, avoids her touch.

JEAN: What's wrong with you, Arlington? I know when you're worrying about something.

ARLINGTON: Just one or two man upset

me, y'know. Just got to break through.

JEAN: You're not getting cold feet about us, are you?

ARLINGTON: I know we got to talk, Jean, but I got a headache right now. Just gimme me a bit a time.

He pecks her on the cheek.

JEAN: If we're gonna make this commitment, Arlington, we've got to learn to communicate. I don't know about you, but as far as I'm concerned, a commitment is for life.

ARLINGTON: *(Shaking)* Just shut up, will you, Jean! Life! What do you know about life? You don't even know the meaning of the word!

JEAN: What did I say?

ARLINGTON: Just leave me alone!

Shaking violently ARLINGTON picks up

his jacket and storms off into the bathroom. He holds onto the sink to stop himself shaking, looks into the mirror, and pauses. He pulls out the contents of his jacket pocket, cigarettes, lighter, loose change, a rock of Crack, etc., and takes a cigarette from the box to light it. He looks at lighter, cigarette, and pauses. He picks up the Crack, looks at himself in the mirror, and back at the Crack. He picks up the toothbrush glass, puts it down nearby, opens the cigarette packet and removes the foil paper. Then he empties the toothbrushes from the glass and rummages around in the bathroom cabinet. Not finding what he wants, he goes to the inside pocket of his jacket, pulls out the gun and puts it on top of the bathroom cabinet. Goes back to the jacket pocket and pulls out a

wad of money tied together with an elastic band. He removes the elastic band, drops the money on the floor, and starts to build a homemade Crack-pipe. In the background, "Songs of Praise" is on the television. He's about to light the pipe, but still shaking; he drops the glass in the sink. Trying instinctively to rescue the Crack, he cuts his hand on the broken glass. MARCUS hears the noise and his father's scream and runs into the bathroom. ARLINGTON shoves him away, getting blood all over MARCUS'S face. In total panic, he grabs hold of MARCUS, rummages in the cabinet, finds the bleach, grabs a towel, pours on the bleach and starts to wipe MARCUS'S face. MARCUS screams.

MARCUS: Dad! Dad! What you doing?

ARLINGTON: Keep still!

MARCUS: Get off me! Mum!

ARLINGTON: Shut up!

MARCUS: Mum!

ARLINGTON: Close your eyes.

MARCUS: Get off me! Get off me!

ARLINGTON: Close your eyes! Come here! Shut up!

MARCUS: Mum! Mum!

JEAN runs into the bathroom, screaming.

JEAN: Don't pour bleach on him! ... Don't pour bleach on him! ... Pour it down the toilet! What the hell do you think you're doing ... have you gone mad?

JEAN knocks the bleach out of ARLINGTON'S hand.

Marcus, wash your face.

MARCUS: There's glass in the sink.

JEAN: Just wash your face and go to your room.

MARCUS: There's glass in the sink.

JEAN: Well, clear it up.

ARLINGTON: I'll clear it up. Just don't touch the blood.

JEAN: Don't tell him, don't touch the blood. Marcus, don't touch the glass.

ARLINGTON: Don't touch the blood.

JEAN: What's this with you and blood? You got some disease or something?

ARLINGTON: Marcus go to your room!

JEAN: Don't you tell him to go to his room. I tell him to go to his room. Marcus, go to your room! *(To Arlington)* You've not been here two minutes, you're screaming down my throat, and bleaching my son like bloody Michael Jackson. Where's that mop?

JEAN storms off to the kitchen, looking for the

**mop, followed by
ARLINGTON.**

ARLINGTON: Jean, listen to me...

JEAN: Don't you ... just don't you
even bother ... If you're
having some kind of nervous
breakdown, Arlington, you
better go have it some place
else, cos I got no time for
sickness ...

ARLINGTON: Well, that's exactly what I'm
talking about...

JEAN: It's just me one and Marcus,
and that's all there is.

ARLINGTON: Jean, I got AIDS.

JEAN: And that's all I care about.

ARLINGTON: You're not listening to me,
Jean.

JEAN: You been outta my life for
almost too long and I don't
want no fuss ... and I don't
want no fights.

ARLINGTON: Jean, I got AIDS.

JEAN: You got what?

ARLINGTON: I got AIDS. I been told I got AIDS. The doctors said I've got AIDS.

JEAN: Well, it's not true. Tell them it's not true. You know doctors like making up stories about black people. You know they like blaming black people for everything. It's racism, that's what it is. Take them to the C.R.E. ... sue the bloody doctors ... sue the hospital.

ARLINGTON: I've got it, Jean. I've got it. It's in my blood.

JEAN: No. No.

ARLINGTON: Jean, I'm not going mad. Why do you think I was using the bleach?

JEAN: Oh, Jesus Christ, Marcus.

ARLINGTON: *(Pause)* I'm sorry.

JEAN: Why didn't you use something?

ARLINGTON: I'm sorry.

JEAN:	You've probably gone and given it to me.
ARLINGTON:	Jean...
	Pause. ARLINGTON walks towards her.
JEAN:	Don't touch me! Just get your stuff out, all right.
ARLINGTON:	Look, Jean...
JEAN:	Don't touch me!
ARLINGTON:	You don't know what you're saying.
JEAN:	I trusted you. Don't touch me! I'll call the police all right - don't touch me.
ARLINGTON:	For what you gonna call the police? Call what police?
JEAN:	I said, keep...
	ARLINGTON grabs hold of her.
ARLINGTON:	Call what police?
JEAN:	*(Screaming)* Haa! Haa! Help ... somebody help! ... This

man's got AIDS, and I don't want him touching me! Heeeeellllpppp!

<u>ARLINGTON slaps her, she goes mad, starts screaming and attacking him with her fists.</u>

Get out! Get out! You wanna harm someone, go harm your dirty street whores, cos you been killing me and I ain't even been knowing it. Just get your stuff and get out of my life. You touch me again, and so help me, I'll kill you.

ARLINGTON: You see you ... you see you...

JEAN: Get out! Leave us alone. I'm just sorry I ever laid in the same bed as you. And as for Marcus, you'll be lucky if you ever see him again.

ARLINGTON: Don't kid yourself.

JEAN: Just go, will you, please. Just go.

<u>ARLINGTON takes up his jacket and walks out.</u>

JEAN pauses, goes to the bathroom, wets a towel, and shouts.

Marcus! Marcus, will you get down here right now.

MARCUS: Yeah. What is it?

JEAN: Don't go near that sink. Come here.

MARCUS approaches cautiously. JEAN looks at him, wipes his face and hands, tries to remove his shirt. MARCUS is embarrassed, pulls away.

MARCUS: Get off me. Go away. What you doing?

JEAN: Marcus, will you stand still, please.

MARCUS: Leave me alone. I wanna go out on my bike.

JEAN: No, you can't. It's too late. It's dark.

MARCUS: I wanna go out on my bike.

JEAN: You can't. It's dark.

MARCUS: I wanna go out on my bike.

JEAN: Marcus, I've told you!

MARCUS: Why can't I go out?

JEAN: Marcus, those who can't hear must feel. Now behave yourself and shut up.

MARCUS: I want to go out.

JEAN: Don't talk to me like that, Marcus! I've told you once.

MARCUS: So what if it's dark? I can look after myself.

JEAN: Just go to your room.

MARCUS: No. I wanna go out on my bike. Dad would let me.

JEAN: Well, your dad isn't ... Marcus, what is this in aid of?

MARCUS: Where's my dad gone?

JEAN: He's gone.

MARCUS: I know he's gone. Where's he gone?

JEAN: He's gone back to his flat, and he's not coming back.

MARCUS: Why?

JEAN: We changed our minds. We're not going to be living together after all.

MARCUS: *(Shouting)* But you promised! You said he was gonna come back and everything was gonna be all right!

MARCUS knocks her books off the table.

JEAN: Stop it! Just stop it! Go to your room!

MARCUS: No wonder dad left you. You're selfish, you are. My dad's gonna die of AIDS, and you threw him out.

JEAN: Marcus, where ... Marcus! Marcus!

MARCUS runs from the room, picks up his

jacket, goes to the bathroom and gets the gun. JEAN follows him.

Marcus. Marcus. Will you come out here, please? Marcus, I just want to talk to you. Marcus, please.

MARCUS bolts from the bathroom, JEAN grabs at him, he drops the gun, both pause, and then MARCUS runs out the front door. JEAN picks up the gun, looks at it, empties the bullets into her pocket, goes to the kitchen, puts the gun down, puts on rubber gloves, cleans up the bathroom, and puts the gun and broken glass in the bin. She puts on her coat, takes out the dustbin bag, ties it up, shuts the door behind her, puts the bag in the rubbish outside, and exits.

Scene Ten

*On the Street, Outside
Arlington's Flat*

**ROSE is pacing up and
down, smoking a
cigarette and hungry for
a fix. JEAN enters, rings
the doorbell, waits, rings
again, and then looks
through the letterbox.**

ROSE: If you're looking for a rock,
he ain't here. I'm looking for
him myself.

JEAN: Looking for who exactly?

ROSE: Arlington.

JEAN: Arlington selling Crack?

ROSE: What's your business with
him then?

JEAN: I got business with him.
(Pause) You haven't seen
him, have you?

ROSE: If I'd seen him, do you think
I'd be standing out here like
a bleeding mad woman

---

	waiting for him to come out his front door?
JEAN:	Typical! Just like him never to be around when you need him. *(Pause)* Look, if you see him, will you tell him that Jean needs to speak to him.
ROSE:	Jean?
JEAN:	'Cos I'm not waiting around all day. Yes.
ROSE:	Are you that little boy's mother?
JEAN:	Why?
ROSE:	No reason.
JEAN:	Yes, I am. Have you seen him?
ROSE:	No, not today. Lovely little boy.
JEAN:	Tell me about it.
ROSE:	I've got no kids. I've had two abortions, though. Want a fag?
JEAN:	No, thanks.

ROSE:	Go on. Have one.
JEAN:	No, thank you!
ROSE:	Don't suppose you got a rock, have you?
JEAN:	What?
ROSE:	All right, keep your wig on!
JEAN:	Who the hell are you, anyway?
ROSE:	Just a friend. Good friend, as it goes.
JEAN:	Really!
ROSE:	Don't take it so seriously, love, I'm just a mate looking for a wrap. What's your problem?
JEAN:	Arlington's my problem. Excuse me.
ROSE:	Who you pushing?
JEAN:	Just clear the way.
ROSE:	Look, I got business with Arlington, okay. Who you

pushing?

JEAN: I'm not looking for an argument with you.

ROSE: Here, just watch who you're pushing.

JEAN: It was an accident. Do you think I'd deliberately want to touch you?

ROSE: Don't come all grand with me, you stuck-up cow, I ain't after your man.

JEAN: Since you and him are such good friends, if you know what's good for you, you'd go and get an AIDS test.

ROSE: What's that supposed to mean?

JEAN: You heard me.

ROSE: Stuck-up cow!

JEAN: Better than being a dried-up whore.

ROSE: Come back here and say that.

JEAN: Why? Are you deaf or

something?

ROSE: Bleeding cheek. And there's
          me trying to be nice to her as
          well.

          **JEAN exits. ROSE steps
          out her cigarette, looks
          through the letterbox
          and shouts.**

ROSE: Arlington! Arlington, if
          you're in there open this
          bleeding door!

          **She lights another
          cigarette, looks up and
          down the street, and
          sees STAGGER, shouts.**

          Stagger! Stagger! Hey,

Stagger!

          **She puts two fingers in
          her mouth and whistles.
          STAGGER turns and
          walks towards her.**

STAGGER: What you after?

ROSE: Oh, Stagger, darling, am I
          glad I've seen you. You don't
          have a wrap, do you?

STAGGER: You have money?

ROSE: Enough for one.

STAGGER: No, my piece too big fe sell fa twenty dollars.

ROSE: Oh, God, no. Come on, Stagger.

STAGGER shakes his head, starts to move off.

I been waiting all day for Arlington, I don't know where he is, have you seen him?

STAGGER: Me nuh see him.

ROSE: Stagger, wait, wait. I think I got something you might want to know.

STAGGER: Like what?

ROSE: What's it worth?

STAGGER: Depends, ennit.

ROSE: Do me a twenty.

STAGGER: Arright. What you have?

ROSE: You'll do it for me?

STAGGER: Come nuh. You t'ink me have time fe game?

ROSE: I hear it from a reliable source. From his little boy's mother. Arlington's got AIDS.

STAGGER: Bombo!

ROSE: I knew you'd wanna know.

STAGGER: Bombo! A me de Don now. Bombo!

STAGGER walks off smiling, and humming to himself, without giving ROSE her fix.

ROSE: Stagger! Stagger! Uncircumcised Baboon! Moron of a frog! Next time find someone else to do it to doggy-fashion. Piiig!

Scene Eleven

Inside Arlington's Flat

ARLINGTON is lying on the settee looking up at the ceiling. A pause. The doorbell rings. ARLINGTON answers it. STAGGER enters, torn, drugged and battered.

STAGGER: Weh you been?

ARLINGTON: I been here today.

STAGGER: Me come pass here this afternoon, y'nuh.

ARLINGTON: This afternoon? This afternoon? No. I was out this afternoon.

STAGGER: Me come pass four o'clock this afternoon, you light off. Me go to the Gambling House, me come back - me see you light on - but you nuh deh 'bout. Me t'ink, you must be taking the Concorde.

ARLINGTON: I was out most of this afternoon.

STAGGER sucks his teeth, goes into the living room, looks around, and sits down.

STAGGER: So wha'appen?

ARLINGTON: Just chilling out, you know.

STAGGER: Yeah?

ARLINGTON: Yeah, man.

STAGGER: So how come you nuh have nuh woman 'bout de place?

ARLINGTON: Me nuh want no woman, man.

STAGGER: No?

ARLINGTON: No, star. Just chilling out.

STAGGER: Me was gonna bring a couple a gyal, y'nuh, an' a couple a rock. Me an' you could lick a rock an' dush a gyal. How come you nuh have nuh woman deh 'bout?

ARLINGTON: What you looking at me like that for, man?

STAGGER: *(Laughs)* Nutten. Bwoy!

**Pause. STAGGER starts
to sing.**

*Come pan de scene in a
Limousine
Gwane like you bad, gwane
like you mean*

*Talk 'bout you big, talk 'bout
you broad*

*Upon mi check it out, you
nutten but a fraud*

*Mi a go bus' a shot
Mi a go fire two shot
Mi a go bus' a shot
Mi a go fire two shot*

ARLINGTON: I see Cooper.

STAGGER: Weh him seh?

ARLINGTON: Say to ring him.

STAGGER: Him have de job still?

ARLINGTON: You could get it, y'know.

STAGGER: Me know me could get it.
You know how long the bitch
been offering me dat job?
T'ree months. Tell him I used
cut hair up in Tottenham

there. I jus' need to brush up on the graduation b'cos back then they didn't have dem new kinda hairstyles.

ARLINGTON: Give him a buzz.

STAGGER: Me nuh want dat job now. Me have bigger t'ings deh pan my mind. *(Sings)* Me a go bus' a shot. Me a go fire two shot.

Pause. STAGGER takes out pipe and crack, starts preparing a draw.

ARLINGTON: What you doing, Stagger, man?

STAGGER: Me have one belly cramp, y'nuh. Ooh! Me feel me haffe lick a rock.

ARLINGTON: Not in here, man.

STAGGER: Nobody nar look.

ARLINGTON: Don't pipe up in here.

STAGGER: Wah wrong wid you? You gone soft?

ARLINGTON: Respect me, man. I said not

in here.

**STAGGER picks up his
gear, begins to walk out.**

ARLINGTON: Where you going?

STAGGER: Toilet.

ARLINGTON: What you going toilet for?

STAGGER: De toilet won't come to me.

ARLINGTON: Sit yourself down.

STAGGER: I wanna lick a piece.

ARLINGTON: Sit you raas down! I said not
in here.

**STAGGER sucks his
teeth, heads for the
bathroom; ARLINGTON
jumps up, and pushes
him against the wall.**

You taking liberties.

STAGGER: You wah fight me?

ARLINGTON: I ain't fighting you, Stagger.
Just get out.

STAGGER pockets the

**gear and pulls out a
knife.**

STAGGER: Come nuh. Come nuh likkle battybwoy. Me hear you have AIDS. You must be battybwoy. Come nuh. A goin' bleed you to raas. A me de Don now.

STAGGER lunges at him, ARLINGTON side steps, goes for his jacket, can't find the gun. STAGGER lunges again, misses, ARLINGTON throws the jacket in his face, STAGGER stumbles, falls, drops the knife. ARLINGTON picks it up, holds it to STAGGER'S throat.

ARLINGTON: Who tell you I got AIDS?

STAGGER: A joke, Don. A joke.

ARLINGTON: Who told you?

STAGGER: Is Rose. Rose. A she tell me.

ARLINGTON: Go on.

STAGGER: Nutten, Don. Nutten. She

seh she hear it from a good sau'ce.

ARLINGTON: Well, you go tell Rose she hear wrong.

STAGGER: Me her you.

ARLINGTON: And if I see your maaga face round here again, I kill you.

ARLINGTON drags STAGGER to the front door, opens it, kicks him out, and slams the door. Stands there a while, looks about the flat, goes into the living room, hunts for the gun; stops, thinks, puts on his jacket, exits.

Scene Twelve
At Home

JEAN is studying. ARLINGTON rings the doorbell, waits, and rings again. JEAN goes to the door.

JEAN: Who is it?

ARLINGTON: Me.

                    Silence.

                    Jean, open the door.

                    Silence. He rings the bell continuously. She doesn't move. He starts to bang on the door. She covers her ears. He pounds louder, starts to kick the door. She puts the security chain on.

JEAN: What do you want?

ARLINGTON: Open the door!

JEAN: There's nothing here for you.

ARLINGTON: Come to get some things and apologise.

JEAN: What for?

ARLINGTON: Must be a million reasons.

JEAN: If you need to apologise for anything you shouldn't have done it in the first place.

ARLINGTON: Can I come in?

Silence. He smashes the small glass panel in the front door, pushes his hand through, opens the lock, and kicks the door off the chain. She's standing before him, screaming and crying.

JEAN: There's nothing here for you! There's nothing here for you! Just go away and leave me alone!

He goes straight into the bathroom, looks on top of the cabinet, rummages through the cabinet, and doesn't find the gun. Goes to the living room where JEAN

is sitting on the settee.

ARLINGTON: I left something in the bathroom. Have you seen it?

She throws the bullets at him.

Where's the rest of it?

JEAN: Ask your son!

ARLINGTON: Where is he?

JEAN: He's quite safe now. Don't you worry about that. As for what you're looking for, you won't find it here. So please just go.

ARLINGTON: Where is it?

JEAN: Just go. You're nothing to do with us. Haven't you caused me enough pain?

ARLINGTON: Listen, Jean, I ain't come here to argue with you. Can't we just talk?

JEAN: Talk! You want to talk? Shall we talk about the injunction I'll be taking out to stop you entering this property again?

The Child Protection Order I'll be applying to the Courts for to prevent you coming anywhere near Marcus? On the grounds of possession of a fire arms, dealing in Crack-Cocaine, dangerous and violent behaviour, shall I go on?

ARLINGTON: You know I never meant for none a that to come near Marcus.

JEAN gives him a 'tough-shit' look.

Jean ... it's me this.

JEAN: There ain't nothing left in this whole world I care about but Marcus. We been doing fine without you up 'til now. I don't need you. He don't need you!

ARLINGTON: He needs a man to show him how to be a man.

JEAN: You? God help us.

ARLINGTON: I'm his dad, Jean.

JEAN: That's just biological.

ARLINGTON: He's my son. And I'm his dad. And if I'm gonna die of AIDS, I wanna see my son.

JEAN: No Judge in his right mind is gonna let you anywhere near him. I'm the working one here, the almost qualified Social Worker; I'm the one constant thing in Marcus life all these years. Where've you been? Fucking your way to AIDS?

ARLINGTON: Bitch!

JEAN: *(Chuckles)* Names can't hurt me, Arlington. You done that. In just one fell swoop, you managed to turn upside down, everything I've accepted all my life. But I bet you never thought you were doing me a favour. It's never too late to change. I know that now. But when it came out, and you told me about this AIDS, yes, I exploded. I blamed it all on you. But it's up to me to protect my own body. It's up to me to take responsibility for my life. And I'll never go back to what I was. I felt hopeless for years living in this flat, but now I've got hope. And if I die tomorrow, I'll never lose that. I used to worry about being lonely. Not having a man in my life. But not now. Now I feel I'm in control. So you do what you have to do. And I'll do what I have to do.

ARLINGTON: I never knew you felt like that.

JEAN: There's a lot you don't know about me.

ARLINGTON: *(Silence)* Look, I'm gonna go. *(Pause)* You know where I am. *(Pause)* We don't need to carry on bad, you know, Jean. We can sort something out. Think about what's best for Marcus. Can I phone you?

JEAN: You can phone him.

ARLINGTON: I'll phone him in a few days' time. *(Pause)* I'll see you then.

JEAN: Yeah.

ARLINGTON: I'm sorry about the door, you hear. Do you want me to get somebody round to fix it?

JEAN: Just ... just ... leave it. I'll sort it out.

ARLINGTON: There's a lot about me you don't know as well, you know.

JEAN: See you.

ARLINGTON turns; hugs her. She stands dead to his embrace. He exits. She closes the door.

Scene Thirteen
In the Park

ARLINGTON and MARCUS are seated on a bench. Music from an ice-cream van can be heard in the distance.

ARLINGTON: Do you realise you had your mother worried to death? *(Pause)* Marcus, I'm talking to you.

MARCUS: What?

ARLINGTON: Don't you know better than not to play with guns?

MARCUS: I wasn't playing with it.

ARLINGTON: What were you doing, then?

MARCUS: I wasn't playing with it ... You shouldn't have it anyway.

ARLINGTON: Marcus, that's not the point, it's for your protection.

MARCUS: Why?

ARLINGTON: Look, there's a lot a people round here don't want work. Want everything but don't wanna do nothing. Some come like animals, break into your house, kill you, take what you have. What I have is mine. I work hard for it and no...

MARCUS: That ain't no way to live.

ARLINGTON: I know that ain't no way to live, but that's life.

MARCUS: So if dog bit you, you gonna bite it back.

ARLINGTON: *(Chuckles)* Marcus, Marcus, Marcus...

MARCUS: If you carried a condom for protection, dad, instead of a gun, you wouldn't have AIDS.

ARLINGTON: Who told you I've got AIDS?

MARCUS: I ain't deaf, you know, I heard you and mum arguing.

ARLINGTON: You're too smart, you know that?

MARCUS: Do you love my mum?

ARLINGTON: Yeah, I love her. I do love her.

MARCUS: But you both said you were gonna live together and be all right.

ARLINGTON: It's not that simple, son. It's just not gonna work out between me and your mum.

MARCUS: Why? Because you've got AIDS?

ARLINGTON: I haven't got AIDS. I've got HIV. I've got the virus that causes AIDS.

MARCUS: Are you a battyman?

ARLINGTON: Don't be stupid, Marcus. 'Course I'm not gay. Anyone can get AIDS, y'know.

MARCUS: Are you gonna die then?

ARLINGTON: Everything dies, you know that. I could get run over by a bus tomorrow. Things get born get old and die.

MARCUS: Yeah, but you're gonna die

young and skinny like them people with AIDS on telly.

ARLINGTON: I don't wanna die. I wanna live to see you grow up.

MARCUS: What if mum dies of AIDS, what if you both die of AIDS, who's gonna look after me?

ARLINGTON: I'm here, for now, y'know, en I? Your mum's here. We're both here.

MARCUS: Yeah, but you're gonna die.

MARCUS starts to cry. ARLINGTON tries to comfort him. MARCUS flinches, pushes him away.

ARLINGTON: Marcus, don't be stupid. It won't rub off, y'know. I'm here for now ... I ain't going nowhere ... and I need you to be strong for me to be strong. Marcus, look at me. Come on. I never really had the kind of father son relationship people supposed to have, y'know, 'cos my old man was a bastard, he really was. I grew up with a lot of stress in the house. I never got to know him. I missed out on a lot, and if I ever wanted to get to know him now, well, he's dead so ... Look, Marcus, there's things I got to sort out in my own head ... I dunno, maybe I should go and see a counsellor ... but I don't wanna treat you like a stranger no more, y'know, 'cos you're my son. And I love you. I never told you that before, but I do ... you're all I've got.

<u>MARCUS turns and hugs him.</u>

Come on. I brought you here for a reason. *(Gives him the keys)* I've got a surprise for you in the boot.

<u>MARCUS jumps up, goes to the car, opens the boot, and finds a computer.</u>

MARCUS: Wow! Dad, is it mine? Is it really mine?

ARLINGTON: Yep.

MARCUS: Wikid! Wait 'til mum sees this. Wow! Thanks, dad.

ARLINGTON: *(Smiling)* Come here a minute.

MARCUS: What is it?

ARLINGTON: Close your eyes and hold out your hand.

MARCUS does so. ARLINGTON places a condom in his outstretched hand.

What's that?

MARCUS: *(Opening his eyes)* Daad!

ARLINGTON: *(Laughing)* You sinking up your face?

MARCUS: What d'you think I am?

ARLINGTON: A condom can save your life. You know how to use one?

MARCUS: 'Course I do.

ARLINGTON: Good! Keep it in your pocket for now.

MARCUS: You're out of order, dad.

                       **ARLINGTON laughs,
                       ruffles his son's hair.**

ARLINGTON: Come on.

                       **ARLINGTON puts his
                       arm round MARCUS.
                       MARCUS puts the
                       condom in his pocket.
                       They walk off.**

THE END